The Little Mermaid

Down in the bluest deeps of the ocean stood the castle of the Sea King. Its walls were made of pink coral and its roof was made of shells.

The Sea King's wife had died years before and he lived in the palace with his old mother, who helped him to bring up his six daughters. They were all beautiful, but the youngest was the loveliest, with skin as soft as petals and eyes as blue as the ocean. Like all the sea people, she had a fish-tail instead of legs.

The little mermaid loved to hear her grandmother tell stories about the world of humans, far above the waves.

"Up there, the forests are green," said Grandmother. "Birds fly about singing pretty songs and wonderful-smelling flowers grow everywhere."

"When can I visit the world of humans?" asked the little mermaid.

"Not yet!" came the reply. "When you're fifteen, you will come of age and then you can swim up and sit on rocks in the moonlight."

"I wish I were fifteen *now!*" she complained. "I'm sure I'm going to love the world up there."

"Oh, it's quite interesting at first," said her sisters, "but you'll soon grow tired of it. Being underwater is best, though humans don't understand that. Why, if they spent more than a minute or so below the surface, they would drown, poor things!"

At long last, the little mermaid's
fifteenth birthday arrived. She kissed
her family goodbye and swam up to the
surface.

The first thing she saw of the upper world was a sunset that turned the clouds red and gold. Nearby was a big ship with three masts. The ship's decks were lined with coloured lamps and the little mermaid could hear laughter and singing. Curious, she swam closer. A friendly wave lifted her so that she could see in through the cabin windows.

She saw many finely dressed people, and the most handsome was a young prince. It was his sixteenth birthday and everybody was celebrating.

The sailors danced on the deck, and hundreds of rockets were fired off into the air. They burst in fiery colours that were reflected in the sea and in the prince's eyes.

The little mermaid stared and stared at the prince. Long after the birthday party ended, she waited, hoping to see him again.

At midnight, a wind blew up and
filled the ship's sails. Lightning crackled
and the wind howled. The ship raced
between waves as high and black as
mountains. The little mermaid
followed, thinking that the storm was
great fun. Then a great wave crashed
down on the ship. It snapped the masts

and tipped the ship over on its side, so that water rushed in.

As the ship sank, the little mermaid remembered that humans could not live underwater. If she did not help the handsome prince, he might drown. Through the screeching wind and lashing waves she searched for him.

A bolt of lightning lit up the sky and the sea, and the little mermaid saw the prince. He had grown so weak that he could hardly swim.

The little mermaid caught him in her arms and kept his head above water. She held him fast all night, and though her arms ached with his weight, she would not let him go.

At dawn, they drifted into a bay where orange and lemon trees grew. Near the shore was a tall white temple. The little mermaid swam across the bay and laid the prince safely on a stretch of soft yellow sand. She kissed his forehead, then swam back out to sea where she could watch without being seen.

Bells rang and a crowd of young girls came out of the temple. One of them ran down to the beach. She shouted with surprise as she almost stumbled over the prince. The sound of her cry woke him. He opened his eyes and smiled at the girl. Other girls came running and together they carried the prince inside the temple.

The little mermaid was glad the prince was safe, but she felt sad as she dived down and returned to her father's palace.

Day after day she swam back to the bay, hoping to catch sight of the prince, but he was never there, and day after day her heart grew heavier.

"Come with us," her sisters said.

Arm in arm, the sisters swam to the surface and showed the little mermaid the palace where the prince lived.

A great marble staircase came down to the water where one of the prince's ships was moored. The little mermaid visited the palace every morning and every evening, swimming up as close to the staircase as she dared. Many times she saw the prince strolling in the moonlight; many times she followed his boat when he went sailing; and each time she saw the prince, the little mermaid loved him more.

"Put him out of your mind!" her
sisters advised. "Humans never fall in
love with mermaids. They think our
beautiful tails are ugly. Of course, the
prince might love you if your tail
turned into legs, but without magic
that would be impossible."

When she heard this, the little
mermaid knew that the only person
who could help her was the sea witch.
She swam away from her father's
palace, past whirlpools and bubbling
mud until she reached the grey sand
desert where the witch lived,
in a house made from
the bones of
drowned sailors.

When the sea witch caught sight of the little mermaid, the witch smiled, showing the barnacles that grew on her teeth.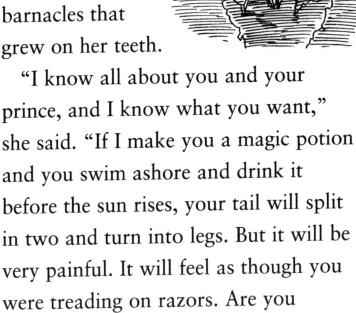

"I know all about you and your prince, and I know what you want," she said. "If I make you a magic potion and you swim ashore and drink it before the sun rises, your tail will split in two and turn into legs. But it will be very painful. It will feel as though you were treading on razors. Are you willing to suffer all this to try and win the prince's love?"

"Yes," whispered the little mermaid.

"But remember," said the witch, "once you have legs, you can never be a mermaid again. And if your precious prince should marry someone else, then the morning after he has married, your heart will break and you will turn into foam on the water."

"I understand," said the little mermaid.

"And the price of my potion is... your voice!" the witch cackled.

"But how can I tell the prince I love him without my voice?" pleaded the little mermaid.

"Make up your mind quickly!" snapped the witch. "Time is growing short!"

The little mermaid nodded her

agreement. The sea witch put her hand over the mermaid's mouth and pulled out her voice by magic; then she brewed the magic potion in a black cauldron.

When it was ready, she poured the potion into a tiny bottle and gave it to the little mermaid.

"You'd better hurry," said the witch. "In the world above, the sky is already getting light."

The little mermaid swam to the surface as fast as she could. By the time she reached the prince's palace, the edge of the sun was showing above the horizon.

She dragged herself on to the bottom of the marble staircase and drank the witch's potion. It burned her throat; she felt as though a sword was cutting her in half and the pain made her faint.

When she woke the
prince was standing at
the top of the stairs,
gazing at her in
amazement. She
blushed and looked
down and saw two
pretty white legs where
her tail had been.

The prince asked who she was and where she was from, but the little mermaid had no voice to answer him. She could only gaze at him sadly with her deep blue eyes. He took her hand and led her to the palace, and though every step felt as though she were walking on needles and knives, she walked gracefully and smiled whenever the prince looked at her.

Inside the palace, the
mermaid was dressed
in a silk gown. The
prince's parents
declared that she
was the greatest
beauty in the
palace and insisted
that she must live
with them as long
as she liked.

At dinner that
evening, when the
royal musicians played, the little
mermaid rose from her place and
danced. Sharp pains darted through
her feet, but she ignored them, moving
as lightly as a feather in the breeze.

She stared at the prince, trying to tell
him with her eyes and her dancing how
much she loved him. Though her
dancing pleased him, he did not guess
what it meant.

As the days went by, the prince seemed to grow more and more fond of the silent stranger he had found and the little mermaid's heart filled with hope, until one morning, when she and the prince were walking together in the palace garden.

"My dear, I've come to you as a friend," he sighed. "I badly need a friend I can talk to. Tomorrow I go on a voyage to another kingdom, to meet a beautiful princess. My parents insist that I must marry her, but how can I? You see, a few months ago I was shipwrecked. The sea washed me up near a temple and a young girl from the temple found me and saved my life.

That was the only time I met her, but I know she is the only girl I could ever love."

"He doesn't know I saved him," the little mermaid thought sadly. "He doesn't know that

I was the one who carried him through the waves to the temple."

"Don't look so sad, my friend," smiled the prince. "I want you to sail with me and cheer me up with your dancing."

It took a day and a night for the prince's ship to reach the harbour. The king and queen and crowds of smiling people greeted the prince.

The cheering crowds parted and the princess appeared.

"Why, it's her!" cried the prince. "She's the girl from the temple who saved me when I was lying nearly dead on the shore! I can't believe it! We must be married at once!"

That afternoon, the church bells rang and the crowds cheered even more loudly as the prince and princess were married in a grand cathedral.

The little mermaid, in a dress of silk and gold, stood close to the prince throughout the wedding, but she saw and heard nothing. She kept on remembering the sea witch's words: "And if your precious prince should marry someone else, then the morning after he has married, your heart will break and you will turn into foam on the water!"

In the evening, the bride and groom set sail for the prince's home. When it grew dark, lamps were lit and the sailors danced. The little mermaid danced with them, dancing for her prince one last time, though he was too busy looking at his lovely wife to notice.

After everyone had gone to bed, the little mermaid stayed on deck, staring down into the dark water. She thought of her father's palace below the waves and how sad it was that she would never return there. Suddenly, she saw the heads of her sisters rise out of the sea. Their hair had been cut short.

"We gave our hair to the sea witch," they said. "In exchange, she gave us this magic knife. Take it and kill the prince, and you will not die. Your tail will grow again and you can dive down into the sea with us! Hurry, that red streak in the sky means the sun will rise soon! Kill the prince and come back to us!"

The little mermaid took the knife from her sisters and hurried to the prince's cabin; but when she opened the door and saw him lying asleep, whispering his bride's name, her heart broke.

She rushed back on deck and hurled the knife far out into the waves that were blood-red with the light of dawn.

The little mermaid threw herself into the sea and felt her body dissolving into foam.

"I shall turn into water," she thought.

"The water will rise up into clouds and fly over the land and fall as rain. The rain will run into rivers and flow back to the sea, over and over again. Wherever my prince is, on land, or sea, or in the air, I shall be with him..."

Then the foam on the water vanished, and there was nothing to be seen except the great ship riding gently through the waves, and the white sea birds circling overhead.

The Princess
and the Pea

When it was time
for the young
prince to be married,
he went off to search
for a wife.

He was a choosy sort
of prince – only a
real princess was
good enough for him!

He travelled the world,
meeting princess after
princess, but every one
he met seemed to have
something that was not
quite right about her.

So, after many months the prince returned home, feeling really miserable.

"This finding a real princess business is trickier than I thought," he told his parents.

One evening, there was a terrible storm. Thunder rumbled, lightning crackled and rain pelted down. Between peals of thunder came the sound of knocking at the palace gate and the king went to answer it.

A young woman was standing outside the palace. She looked awful. The wind had teased and tangled her hair and she was so wet that rain ran down the back of her neck all the way to her shoes, so that her feet squelched when she walked. The young woman said that she was a princess and asked if she could stay the night.

"*Her?* A *real* princess?" said the queen when she caught a glimpse of their guest. "I'll soon see about that!"

The queen went off to the visitor's bedroom, pulled the mattress and all the sheets and blankets off the bed and put a pea at the bottom. Then she piled twenty mattresses on the pea and stacked twenty thick duvets on top of the mattresses.

The young woman spent the night on this peculiar bed, and in the morning the queen asked if she had slept well.

"No!" groaned the young woman. "The bed was so uncomfy! There was a hard lump in the middle that stuck into me so much, I didn't sleep at all. I'm covered in bruises!"

Now the queen knew for certain that the young woman was a princess, because she had felt the pea through twenty mattresses and twenty duvets.

"Only a *real* princess would have such delicate skin," the queen told her son.

"A real princess at last!" gasped the prince. "My search is over!"

And so the prince married the princess, and the pea was put on show in the Royal Museum. It's still there – unless someone has stolen it.

And that's a *real* story for you!